COLUMBIA PICTURES PRESENTS A MARVEL ENTERPRISES PRODUCTION A LAURA ZISKIN PRODUCTION 'SPIDER-MAN'
STARRING: TOBEY MAGUIRE WILLEM DAFOE KIRSTEN DUNST JAMES FRANCO CLIFF ROBERTSON ROSEMARY HARRIS
MUSIC BY DANNY ELFMAN EXECUTIVE PRODUCERS AVI ARAD STAN LEE SCREENPLAY BY DAVID KOEPP BASED ON THE MARVEL COMIC BOOK BY STAN LEE PRODUCED BY LAURA ZISKIN IAN BRYCE DIRECTED BY SAM RAIMI

MARVEL

sony.com/Spider-Man

COLUMBIA
PICTURES

HarperCollins®, HarperFestival®, and Festival Readers™ are trademarks of
HarperCollins Publishers Inc.

Library of Congress Catalog Card Number: 2001092287

6 7 8 9 10

❖

First Edition

www.harperchildrens.com
GO FOR THE ULTIMATE SPIN AT
www.sony.com/Spider-Man

I Am Spider-Man

Adaptation by Acton Figueroa

Based on the screenplay by David Koepp

Illustrations by Ron Lim

Coloring by Emily Y. Kanalz

📖 HarperFestival®

A Division of HarperCollins*Publishers*

Maybe you've heard of me.

Maybe you've seen me.

I am Spider-Man.

I wasn't always a superhero. I used to be a regular guy, just like everyone else. Well, not exactly like everyone else.

I was sort of a geek.

I really liked school.

But it wasn't always easy for me.

I didn't always fit in.

Some of the kids didn't like me.

Everything changed

when we went on a field trip

to learn about spiders.

Man-made spiders. Super-spiders.

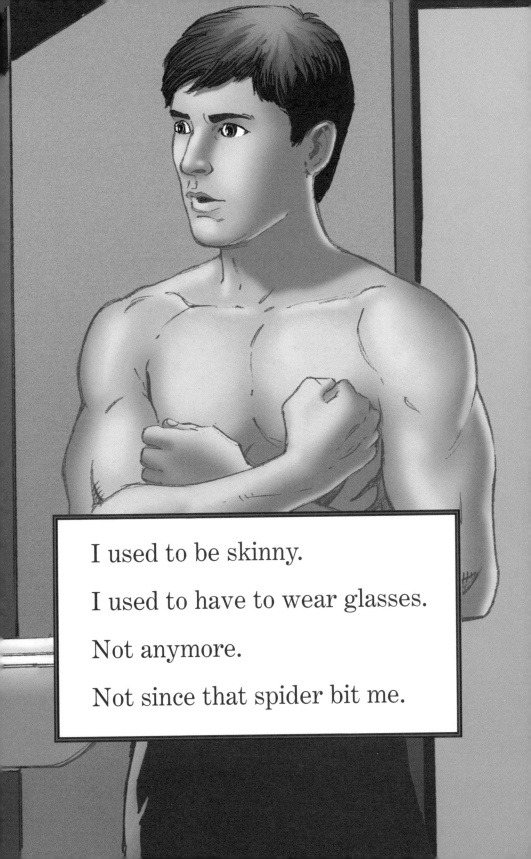

I used to be skinny.

I used to have to wear glasses.

Not anymore.

Not since that spider bit me.

Now I am fast.

Now I am strong.

The kids at school were amazed at my new strength.

Like the spider that bit me,
I have an extra sense.
My spider sense warns me
when someone needs my help.

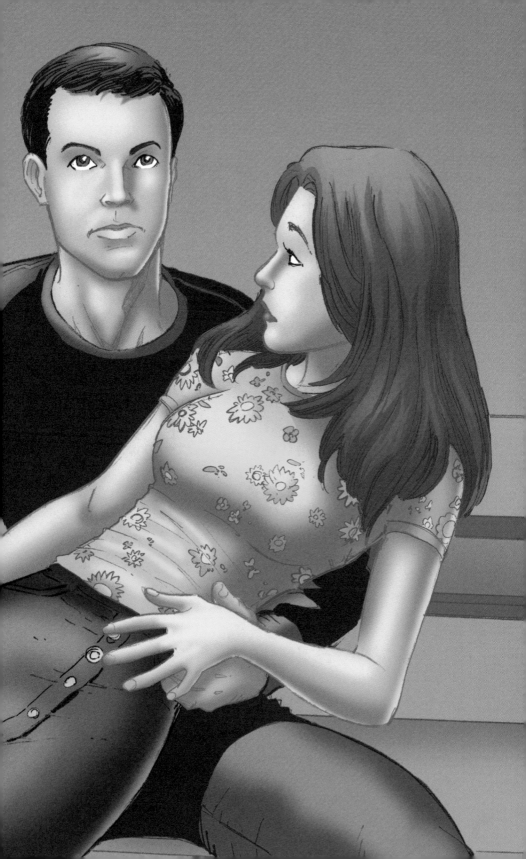

After the spider bit me,

I began to make webbing.

At first I couldn't control it.

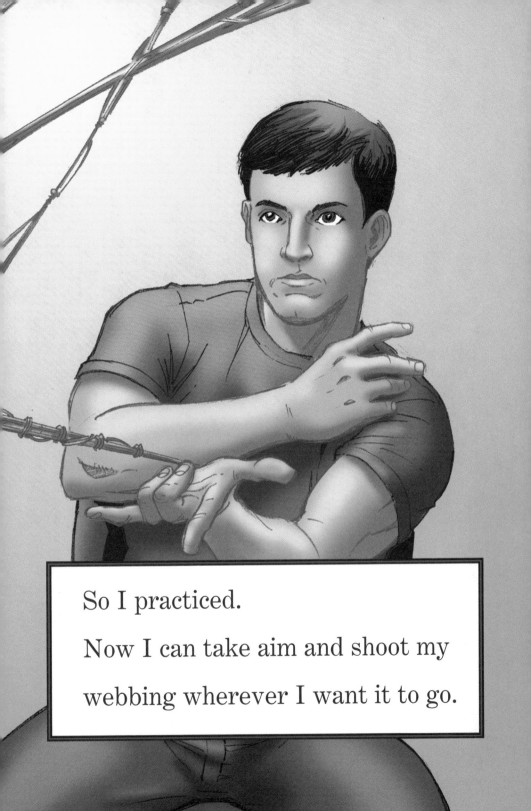

So I practiced.

Now I can take aim and shoot my webbing wherever I want it to go.

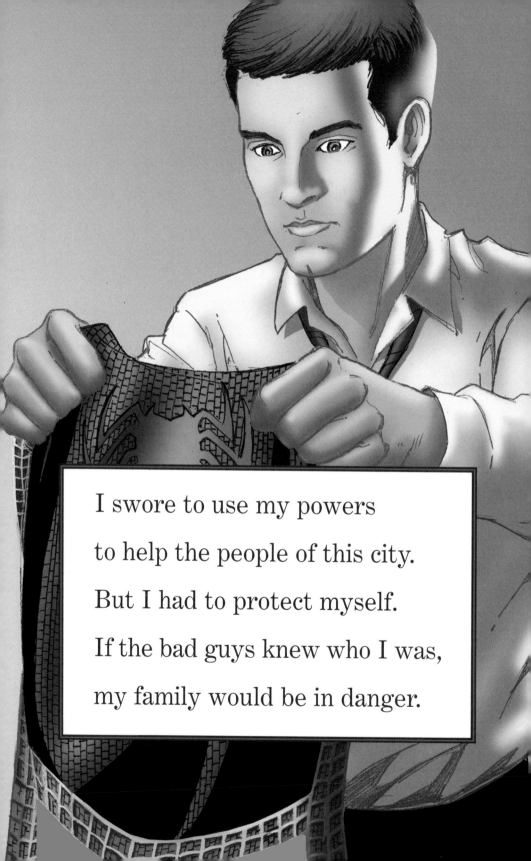

I swore to use my powers
to help the people of this city.
But I had to protect myself.
If the bad guys knew who I was,
my family would be in danger.

And so I became Spider-Man.

Like a spider, I can climb walls.

My fingers can stick to anything.

I can swing through the city
on a strand of webbing.

I can flip, dip, and whirl.

I am strong enough

to fight four bad guys at once!

I can go places no one else can.

As Spider-Man,

I am always on the lookout for evil.

Sometimes it comes looking for me.

I'll always be Peter Parker.

But when people are in danger,

I *am* Spider-Man.